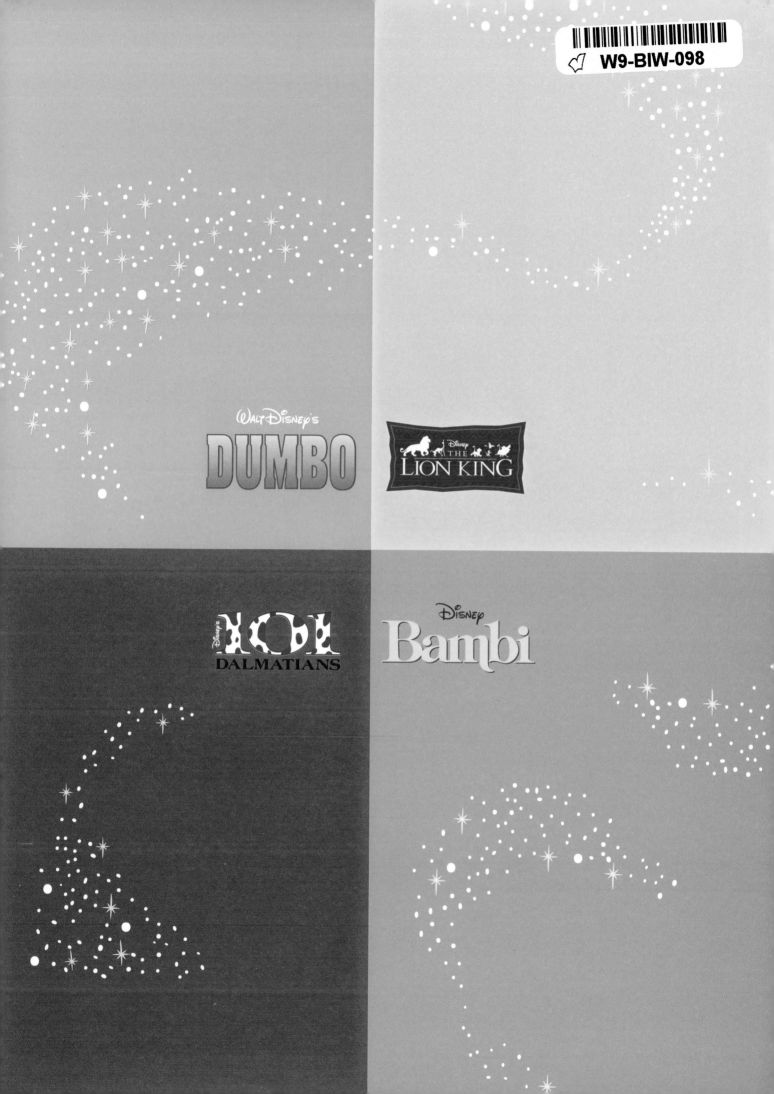

WALT DISNEY'S
DUMBO

Disney
THE
LION KING

Disney's
101
DALMATIANS

Disney
Bambi

Disney Animals
CD STORYBOOK

Disney Animals
CD STORYBOOK

The Lion King
101 Dalmatians
Bambi
Dumbo

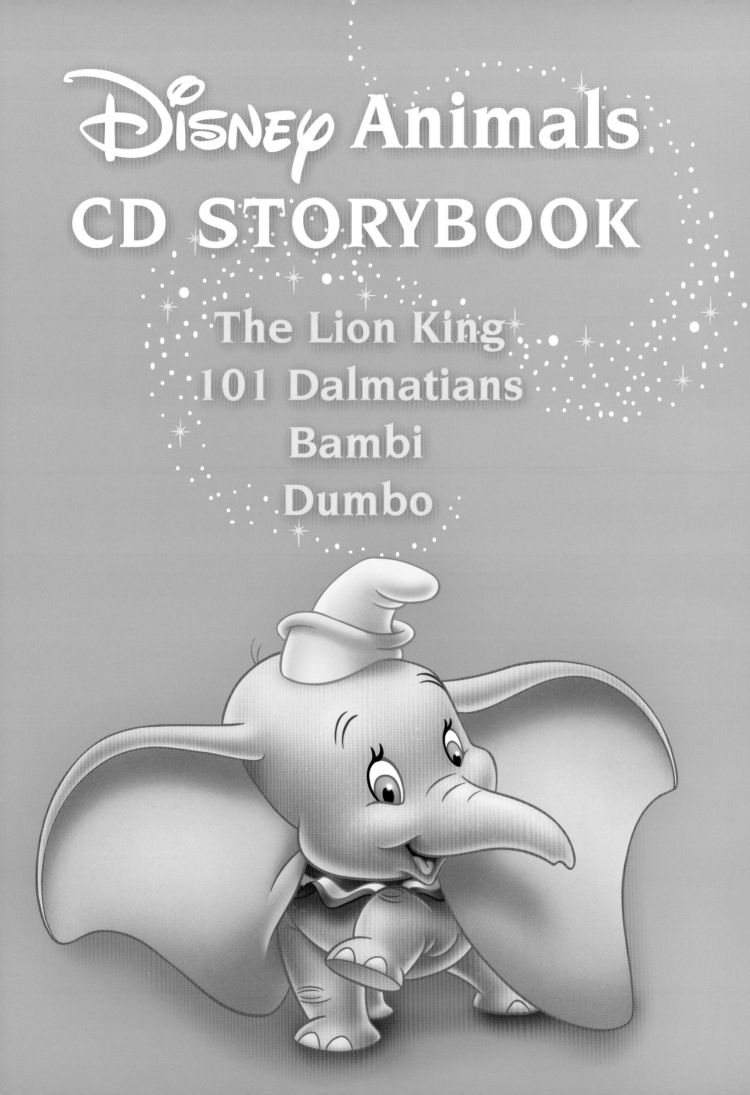

Hinkler Books Pty Ltd 2005
17-23 Redwood Drive
Dingley, VIC, 3172
www.hinklerbooks.com
Reprinted 2005

© Disney Enterprises, Inc.

101 Dalmatians, Bambi and Dumbo adapted by Karen Comer
Book design by Hinkler Design Studio

ISBN 1 7412 1922 1

Printed and manuctured in China.

Disney Animals
CD STORYBOOK

Contents

Every morning, as the sun peeked over the horizon, a giant rock formation caught the first rays of light. This was Pride Rock, home to King Mufasa and his lovely wife, Queen Sarabi.

On this particular morning, animals from all over the Pride Lands had journeyed to Pride Rock to honor the birth of the newborn cub, Simba.

As part of the celebration, Rafiki had a special duty. He cracked open a gourd, dipped his finger inside and made a mark on Simba's forehead. Then Rafiki lifted the future king up high for all to see.

The elephants trumpeted with their trunks, giraffes bowed their heads and the zebras stamped their hooves with approval.

Not far from the ceremony, in a cave at the back side of Pride Rock, a scraggly lion with a dark mane grumbled. "Life's not fair. I shall never be King." This was Mufasa's brother, Scar, who was jealous of Simba's position as the next king.

Moments later, Mufasa was at the doorway to Scar's cave. "Sarabi and I didn't see you at the presentation of Simba," he said.

Zazu, Mufasa's trusted advisor, also appeared. "You should have been first in line," he said. "I was first in line until the little hairball was born," Scar replied. And with that, he stalked out of the cave.

Before long, Simba grew into a healthy, playful young cub. Early one morning, he and Mufasa climbed to the top of Pride Rock. As they looked out at the rising sun, Mufasa pointed across the Pride Lands. "Look, Simba: Everything the light touches is our kingdom."

Simba scanned the horizon and noticed a dark spot in the distance. "What about that shadowy place?"

"That's beyond our borders. You must never go there, Simba," said Mufasa.

"But I thought a king can do whatever he wants," Simba said.

"There's more to being king than getting your way all the time," said Mufasa. "Everything you see exists together in a delicate balance. As king you need to understand that balance and respect all the creatures—from the crawling ant to the leaping antelope. We are all connected in the great Circle of Life."

Later, as Simba headed back down the path, he ran into Scar. "Hey, Uncle Scar! Guess what? I'm gonna be King of Pride Rock. My dad just showed me the whole kingdom! And I'm gonna rule it all!"

Scar looked slyly at the young cub. "He didn't show you what's beyond that rise at the northern border?"

"Well, no. He said I can't go there," said Simba.

"And he's absolutely right. It's far too dangerous," said Scar. "Only the bravest lions go there. Promise me you'll never visit that dreadful place."

When Simba returned home, he found his friend Nala and her mother, Serafina, visiting with Sarabi. "Come on! I just heard about this great place!"

The mothers gave permission for the youngsters to go exploring, as long as Zazu went with them. Simba and Nala raced across the Pride Lands in an effort to lose the watchful bird. They led him through many herds of animals until they finally lost him.

Once the cubs were free of Zazu, Simba pounced on Nala, then Nala flipped Simba onto his back. They tumbled down a hill and landed in a dark ravine littered with elephant skulls and bones.

Simba looked around and gasped. "This is it! We made it!"

Before the cubs could explore any farther, Zazu tracked them down. "We're way beyond the boundary of the Pride Lands. And right now we are all in very real danger."

Suddenly, three hyenas slithered out of the eye sockets of an elephant skull. Frightened, Simba, Zazu, and Nala jumped back.

The hyenas, Banzai, Shenzi, and the always-laughing Ed, eyed them greedily.

Banzai sneered. "A trio of trespassers."

Zazu tried to lead the cubs to safety, but Banzai grabbed him by the neck and plopped him down. The hyenas circled their prey, licking their chops.

"What's the hurry? We'd love you to stick around for dinner."

While the hyenas argued about who was going to eat whom, Simba, Nala, and Zazu quietly slipped away. But the hyenas weren't distracted for long. They gave chase, and Simba and Nala had to run as fast as they could. Finally, they tried hiding behind some elephant bones.

Just when it looked as if it were all over for the young cubs, Mufasa appeared and sent the hyenas flying with a swipe of his big paw. "If you ever come near my son again . . ."

The hyenas slinked away, and Mufasa glared at Simba.

"You deliberately disobeyed me! I'm very disappointed in you!"

Mufasa sent Nala and Zazu home so he could talk privately to his son.
Simba peered up at his father.

"I was just trying to be brave, like you," he said.

"Being brave doesn't mean you go looking for trouble," said Mufasa.
"Dad, we're pals, right? And we'll always be together, right?"

Mufasa looked up at the stars. "Simba, let me tell you something my
father told me: Look at the stars. The great kings of the past look down
on us from those stars. So whenever you feel alone, just remember that
those kings will always be there to guide you. And so will I."

Meanwhile, the hyenas received another visitor: an angry Scar showed up at their lair. "I practically gift-wrapped those cubs and you couldn't even dispose of them."

Scar warned the hyenas to be prepared.

Banzai laughed. "Yeah! Be prepared. We'll be prepared! . . . For what?"

Scar looked at him with danger in his eyes. "For the death of the king."

The following day, Scar invited Simba to join him in the gorge.

When they arrived, Scar turned to his young nephew. "Now you wait here. Your father has a marvelous surprise for you."

Moments after he left, Scar signaled the hyenas, who chased a herd of wildebeests directly toward Simba.

From a distance, Mufasa noticed the rising dust. Scar appeared quickly at his side.

"Stampede! In the gorge! Simba's down there!"

Without waiting a second, Mufasa took off to save his young son.

Mufasa plunged into the gorge and battled his way through the oncoming wildebeests. He found Simba, grabbed him by the nape of his neck, and put him on a nearby ledge. Suddenly, Mufasa was knocked back into the stampede.

Desperately, he tried to climb up another ledge from which Scar stood looking down on him. "Brother—help me!" cried Mufasa.

Scar reached for Mufasa and pulled him close enough to whisper in his ear. "Long live the King." Then Scar let go of Mufasa and he fell to his death. Simba peered over the ridge just as his father disappeared beneath the thundering stampede.

Later, Scar found Simba hovering over his father's body, sobbing. "It was an accident. I didn't mean for it to happen."

"But the king is dead," said Scar. "And if it weren't for you, he'd still be alive. Oh, what will your mother think?"

Simba sobbed harder. "What am I going to do?"

"Run away, Simba. Run! Run away and never return."

Simba did as he was told, unaware that his uncle's hyena friends had been ordered to finish him off. Scar returned to Pride Rock to take over the throne.

Meanwhile, Simba plodded across the savannah without any food or water. It wasn't long before he fainted under the hot sun.

As the vultures circled overhead, a big-hearted warthog named Pumbaa stumbled upon the young lion. He turned to his trusty pal, a fast-talking meerkat named Timon. "He's so cute and all alone. Can we keep him?"

"Pumbaa, are you nuts? Lions eat guys like us." But Pumbaa scooped Simba up anyway and carried him to safety.

When Simba awoke, the first thought that sprang to mind was his father's death. Timon taught him about *hakuna matata*, which means no responsibilities, no worries.

"You've got to put your past behind you," Timon explained.

And that is exactly what Simba did. He stayed in the jungle with Pumbaa and Timon a long, long time, and grew into a very big lion. But eventually he became homesick. One night he looked up at the stars and recalled the words his father had told him long ago.

"The great kings of the past look down on us from those stars.

So, whenever you feel alone, just remember that those kings will always be there to guide you. And so will I."

The next day, Pumbaa was chased by a lioness.

Simba came to his rescue but, after wrestling with the lioness, who easily flipped him onto his back, he realized that she was his old friend. "Nala? What are you doing here?" he asked her.

"Why didn't you come back to Pride Rock? You're the king!" Nala replied.

"I'm not the king. Scar is."

"Simba, he let the hyenas take over the Pride Lands."

"What?"

"There's no food, no water. If you don't do something soon, everyone will starve. You're our only hope," Nala told him.

"I can't go back," Simba yelled at the heavens. He missed Mufasa terribly. "You said you'd always be there for me, but you're not . . . because of me."

Simba didn't believe he could challenge Scar for the throne, so he stayed in the jungle with Nala and his new friends. But Rafiki knew the time had come for Simba to take his place in the Circle of Life, and he headed for the jungle.

When Simba saw Rafiki, he was surprised. "Who are you?"

"The question is: 'Who are you?'" said Rafiki.

"I thought I knew. Now I'm not so sure," Simba replied.

"Well, I know who you are. You're Mufasa's boy. He's alive, and I'll show him to you. You follow old Rafiki. He knows the way."

Rafiki led Simba to a reflecting pool. When he looked into the water, he saw a lion. "That's not my father. It's just my reflection."

"Look harder . . . You see, he lives in you."

The ghost of Mufasa magically appeared. "Look inside yourself, Simba. You are more than what you have become. You must take your place in the Circle of Life."

Encouraged by his father's words, Simba returned to Pride Rock. Nala, Pumbaa, and Timon followed. When Simba arrived, he found the land bare and dry. The hyenas were in control and Scar was shouting at Simba's mother.

Sarabi turned to Scar. "We must leave Pride Rock." She explained that there was no food left.

"We're not going anywhere. I am the king," said Scar.

"If you were half the king Mufasa was—"

"I AM TEN TIMES THE KING MUFASA WAS!"

Suddenly, a flash of lightning revealed the edge of Pride Rock, and there stood Simba. Scar jumped back.

"Simba . . . I'm a little surprised to see you . . . alive."

"Give me one good reason why I shouldn't rip you apart."

But Scar forced Simba to say, in front of all the lions, that he had caused his father's death.

Scar smirked. "Oh, Simba, you're in trouble again. But this time Daddy isn't here to save you. And now everyone knows why."

Simba backed up against the ledge. Lightning struck again, setting fire to the dry brush of the Pride Lands.

Simba leapt on Scar. Nala and the other lionesses joined the battle. Through the smoke and flames of the brushfire, Simba spotted Scar trying to escape and he ran after the old lion. Scar pleaded with his nephew. "Simba, I'll make it up to you. I promise. How can I prove myself to you?"

"Run. Run away, Scar, and never return."

Scar started to slink off, but then he turned and lunged one last time at Simba. Simba moved quickly and flipped Scar over the ledge, where a pack of hyenas was waiting hungrily.

Limping badly, Simba climbed up to the very top of Pride Rock. He let out a magnificent roar as he looked out over his kingdom.

Before long, Pride Rock flourished again. Nala remained by Simba's side, and soon they had their own newborn cub. With all their friends around, including Zazu, Pumbaa and Timon, a new celebration of life took place. After making a mark on the forehead of the young cub, Rafiki held him up for all the kingdom to see. The Circle of Life continued.

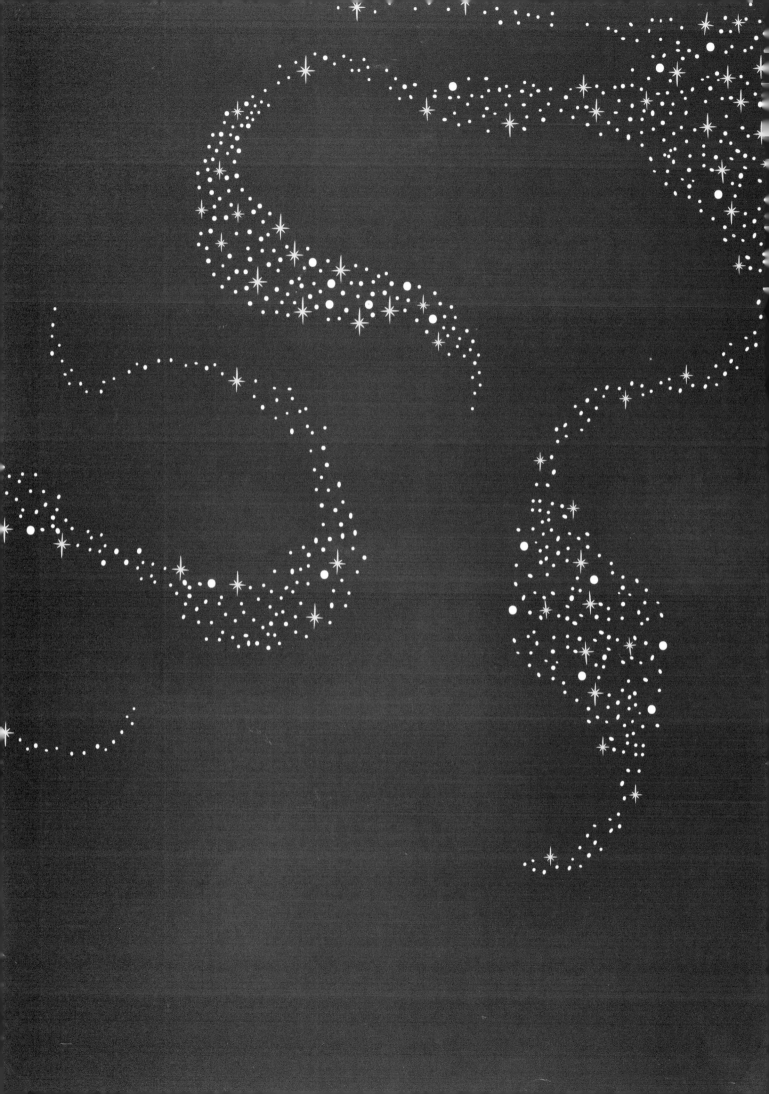

It was a beautiful spring day in London. Pongo sat thinking about how a bachelor's life was downright dull. His owner Roger was a musician, who wrote songs about romance, something Roger knew nothing about.

Roger needed a mate. He was intelligent and handsome, and Pongo was determined to find someone for Roger.

Pongo looked out the window from their house in Regent's Park. He saw a number of dogs and their female owners, but none of them were quite right for Roger—too unusual, too fancy, too old or too young.

Then Pongo saw a Dalmatian—the most beautiful creature on four legs—walking past. Her owner was quite lovely, too. It looked like they were headed for the park.

36

Pongo checked the clock on the mantelpiece. It was half past four. Roger never stopped working until five o'clock. Pongo pushed the hands of the clock forward until the time showed five-fifteen, grabbed his leash, barked at Roger and jumped frantically at the door. Roger stretched and yawned at the piano and checked the clock. "Hmm! After five already—fancy that! All right, Pongo! All right, boy!" he said.

Pongo dragged Roger to the park, desperately searching for the Dalmatian and her owner.

At last Pongo saw them, sitting quietly on a bench. He knew he couldn't depend on Roger, it was all up to him. Pongo wasn't really sure how to attract the female's attention, but he had to try something. He snatched Roger's hat and ran away with it. "Pongo, you silly old thing, come on!" cried Roger.

Pongo dropped Roger's hat onto the bench, but then the Dalmatian and her owner left. Pongo had to try something else—he was determined that Roger and the lovely lady must meet.

Pongo pulled Roger to his feet and pushed him into the lady. Then he ran around and around, binding them together with his leash. They were forced to hold onto one another to try and keep their balance. But they fell into the pond!

"Oh, oh! My new spring suit!" the lady cried. "And my new hat!"

Roger helped her up. "I'm terribly sorry," he apologized.

"Please, just go away, you've done enough," she moaned.

She pulled out her handkerchief to dry her face, but it was dripping with water. Roger pulled out his handkerchief to offer her, but it was just as wet. At this, the lady started to laugh helplessly, and Roger joined in. Pongo and the other Dalmatian simply smiled at each other.

Soon Roger married Anita, the lovely lady from the pond. And Pongo settled down with her Dalmatian, Perdita. They all lived together in a modest little place just right for two couples starting out. They had a wonderful cook and housekeeper, Nanny, who looked after them.

It was not long before Perdita and Pongo were expecting puppies.

One day, while Roger was working on a song, they heard a loud car horn outside. "It's that devil woman!" exclaimed Perdita.

Cruella De Vil, Anita's old schoolmate, appeared at the door. She looked around the house impatiently, asking, "Where are they? Where are they?"

"The puppies won't be here for three weeks," explained Anita. She tried to distract Cruella. "Isn't that a new fur coat?"

"My only true love, darling. I live for furs, I worship furs!" cried Cruella. "I've got to run, darling. Let me know when the puppies arrive." And she left, slamming the door behind her.

It was a wild, stormy night when the puppies were born. Roger and Pongo waited nervously outside the door, while Nanny and Anita helped Perdita.

"Eight puppies!" called out Nanny.

Roger and Pongo danced around. "Why, Pongo boy, that's marvellous!" exclaimed Roger. "Ten! Eleven! Thirteen! Fourteen! Fifteen! Fifteen puppies!"

Then Nanny came out, with a tiny bundle covered in a blanket. "Fourteen," she said sadly. "We lost one."

She gave the small bundle to Roger. "Oh, Pongo boy. And yet I wonder," mused Roger. He rubbed the little puppy in the blanket.

More thunder crashed. Pongo watched anxiously.

All of a sudden, a little nose wriggled from underneath the blanket. "Look, Pongo! Fifteen!" cried Roger excitedly.

Another crash of thunder, and suddenly Cruella was at the door. "How marvellous!" she cried.

She looked at the puppy in Roger's hands and noticed that it was completely white. "No spots at all! What a horrid little white rat!" she spat.

Nanny explained defensively that the puppies would have their spots in a few weeks.

"I'll take them all!" Cruella declared, spraying Roger and Pongo with ink as she readied her pen and checkbook. "Just name your price, dear."

"I'm afraid we can't give them up," said Anita. "Poor Perdy. She'd be heartbroken."

"You can't possibly afford to keep them, you can scarcely feed yourselves!" Cruella said, laughing cruelly.

Roger bravely insisted that they would not sell the puppies.

"I'll get even. You'll be sorry! You fools!" hissed Cruella and she left, slamming the door behind her.

The puppies grew up, watched closely by Pongo and Perdita. They loved watching television, especially a cartoon show about a hero dog called Thunderbolt.

"He's even better than Dad!" said Patch.

"No dog's better than Dad!" replied Penny.

"I'm hungry, Mother," complained Rolly.

The show finished, and Pongo and Perdita bundled the puppies off to bed.

Roger, Anita, Pongo and Perdita went out for their evening walk. As they strolled down their street, two men watched them from a van. Jasper was the tall, thin man; the other was Horace, short and stout.

Horace muttered, "I don't like it, Jasper. I want to get out of this job. I don't like it."

"Let's get on with it, Horace me lad," said Jasper.

The van rolled to the front of Roger and Anita's house.

Nanny had just finished putting the puppies to bed, when the doorbell rang. Jasper and Horace were at the door, claiming to be from the electric company.

Nanny dismissed them, but they forced their way in. She tried to stop them, but they were too strong for her. When they left, Nanny realized they had taken the puppies. "Those scoundrels! They stole the puppies! Help! Help! Help!" she cried.

The newspapers had headlines about the stolen puppies. Cruella laughed as she read them.

The phone rang. "Jasper! How dare you call me here?" Cruella shouted into the phone.

"We don't want no more of this here. We'll settle for half," Jasper said.

"Not one shilling until the job's done," Cruella cried.

"I don't like it, Jasper," Horace muttered.

"Ah, shut up!" Jasper said as he turned to Horace.

"What? Why, you imbecile!" shouted Cruella, hanging up the phone.

Although Scotland Yard had been called in to help, Pongo realized the humans couldn't help. "Perdy, I'm afraid it's all up to us. Darling, there's the Twilight Bark—the very fastest way to send news."

So on their evening walk, Pongo barked out the news about their missing puppies. No one answered and Perdita despaired of anyone listening.

"We've got to keep trying, Perdy," insisted Pongo.

Pongo eventually reached the Great Dane at Hampstead before Roger and Anita dragged them home.

The Great Dane passed on the news about the missing puppies from dog to dog. The barking continued all over the city.

"It's an all dog alert!"

"Fifteen Dalmatian puppies, stolen."

"The humans have tried everything. Now it's up to us dogs and the Twilight Bark."

The barking spread from the city to the country.

The barking reached a horse named Captain. "It's an alert," he realized.

Captain woke up Sergeant Tibs, a tabby cat, who woke up the Colonel, an English Sheepdog.

"What's the word, Colonel?" asked Captain.

"It's from London," he replied.

They tried to decode the message and eventually worked out that fifteen puppies had been stolen.

Tibs remembered hearing barking coming from De Vil Hall close by, even though no one had lived there for years. There was even smoke coming from the chimney.

Sergeant Tibs and the Colonel decided to check out De Vil Hall, even though the old place was said to be haunted.

Tibs crept through a hole in the wall, and saw an astonishing sight. There inside the room were lots and lots of Dalmatian puppies. He asked one puppy, "Are you one of the fifteen stolen puppies?"

The puppy explained, "Oh no, we're bought and paid for. There's ninety-nine of us altogether. But there's a bunch of little ones with names and collars."

Tibs started counting the puppies with collars, who were huddled in front of the television. He tried to stay out of sight of Jasper and Horace, who were watching their favorite show.

"Thirteen, fourteen, fifteen!"

Just then, Jasper saw Tibs and grabbed him. He threw Tibs to the other side of the room, hurling an empty bottle after him.

Back in London, the Great Dane met Pongo and Perdita at Primrose Hill with news. The puppies had been located in Suffolk. The Dane gave them instructions, and then added, "If you lose your way, contact the barking chain."

Without a moment's pause, Pongo and Perdita headed off into the snowy night.

Meanwhile, Cruella arrived at De Vil Hall. She snarled at Jasper and Horace, "It's got to be done tonight. The police are everywhere."

Horace replied, "But they ain't big enough!"

Jasper added pleadingly, "You couldn't get half a dozen coats . . ."

Tibs froze. "Coats . . . dog skin coats!"

"Do it—do it now! I want those dog skin coats!" Cruella ordered and left.

Tibs called in a whisper to the puppies. "Hey, kids! You'd better get out of here if you want to save your skins."

The puppies started pushing through the hole in the wall, all except Lucky, that is. He was still watching television, entranced.

"Hey kid, let's go," Tibs whispered.

But Lucky stood up in front of the television, blocking the screen. Jasper threw him aside, and Tibs scooped him up and pushed him through the hole, where Rolly was still trying to fit through.

The television show finished, and Jasper and Horace started arguing about the job. "I'll pop them on the head. You do the skinning," decided Jasper.

"Ah, no you don't, Jasper. I'll pop them off and you do the skinning," Horace argued.

All of a sudden, Jasper and Horace discovered the puppies had disappeared! They took up torches and tracked the puppies up the stairs.

"Come on out!" Jasper called out encouragingly, while he and Horace peered into the rooms with their torches.

The puppies stampeded out from a bedroom, and rushed down the stairs. Jasper and Horace collided in their efforts to catch the puppies. Tibs and the puppies hid under the stairs, trembling with fear, while Jasper and Horace came down the stairs.

Meanwhile, Pongo and Perdita had stopped. "I'm afraid we're lost," cried Perdita.

But just then the Colonel found Pongo and Perdita. "No time to explain, there's trouble!" he cried, and they all ran to De Vil Hall.

Inside, Jasper and Horace cornered the puppies, where Tibs tried valiantly to defend them. Just when it seemed there was no hope, Pongo and Perdita crashed through the window, snarling at Jasper and Horace. Jasper and Horace brandished long clubs, trying to hit Pongo and Perdita.

Tibs called out to the Colonel, "Retreat! Retreat!" and the puppies began to escape outside, following the Colonel.

Perdita pulled up the rug Horace was standing on, and Horace tripped and fell backwards into the fire. He jumped up with a fright and landed against the wall, followed by Jasper, as plaster from the ceiling fell down around them.

Pongo and Perdita were united with their puppies in the shed with the Colonel, Captain and Tibs. "Oh my darlings!" cried Perdita.

"Oh Daddy!" said Patch happily.

"Did you bring us anything to eat?" asked Rolly.

Pongo was overjoyed. "Ha, everybody here? All fifteen?"

"Twice that many, Dad. Now there's ninety-nine of us," answered Patch.

"Ninety-nine?" exclaimed Perdita. "What on earth would she want with so many?"

"She's gonna make coats out of us," whimpered Lucky.

"We've got to get back to London," Pongo decided. "Perdy, we'll take them home with us, all of them."

Perdita thanked Captain, the Colonel and Tibs for their help. "Bless you all."

As Jasper and Horace drove up in their van, Pongo and Perdita led the puppies out the back way. Captain kicked his back legs at Jasper and Horace, and they landed against the wall, while the puppies made their escape.

Jasper and Horace jumped quickly back in their van, following puppy tracks in the snow.

But Pongo and Perdita with their puppies were hidden under a bridge, over the frozen river bed.

The puppies wearily made their way through the snow, Pongo counting them to make sure there were ninety-nine puppies.

"I'm tired, and I'm hungry and my tail's froze . . ." complained Lucky.

Just then a Collie bounded up. "We have shelter for you at the dairy farm," he told a relieved Pongo.

Perdita and Pongo followed the Collie into the dairy barn, with the exhausted puppies, trailing behind.

Within minutes, the puppies had been fed by four kindly cows, and were fast asleep.

Pongo and Perdita led the puppies to the village of Dinsford, where a Labrador was waiting for them. "Pongo, I've got a ride home for you," said the Labrador. "There's a truck going to London after the engine is repaired."

The Dalmatians waited in an old blacksmith shop.

But Cruella in her car, and Jasper and Horace in their van, had tracked the puppies to Dinsford.

As Cruella drove past the shop, Pongo and Perdita wondered how they would get the puppies into the truck.

Lucky and Patch began to play around in the fireplace soot. Pongo had an idea. He told the puppies to roll in the soot so they would look like Labradors—all black and no spots.

"You mean, you want us to get dirty?" Freckles asked in disbelief.

The puppies rolled in soot, and Pongo, Perdita and the Labrador led the puppies out.

Pongo led the last line of puppies into the truck. Snow from a ledge above them dripped onto one of the puppies, melting the soot and revealing his white coat with spots.

Cruella saw this from her car. "It can't be; it's impossible." Cruella realized that the pup was a Dalmatian.

Pongo picked up the last puppy and leapt for the truck, which had started to move. The Labrador snarled at Jasper and Horace, keeping them away from the truck.

Cruella chased the truck in her car, trying to run it off the road. Instead, the truck continued over a bridge, and Cruella was forced off the edge of the road, down into the gully.

Jasper and Horace continued the chase as Cruella drove her smashed car back on the road. She caught up to the truck and rammed her car into it. The truck and Cruella's car veered erratically all over the road.

Then, Jasper and Horace's van swerved into Cruella's car, and the car and van rolled down the valley in pieces.

"You fools!" Cruella sobbed.

Back in London, Roger was listening to his new song on the radio while Anita decorated the Christmas tree.

"I can't believe Pongo and Perdy would run away," Roger sighed.

Nanny bustled in. "Sometimes at night I can hear them barking, but it always turns out I'm dreaming."

Suddenly there was barking, and Pongo and Perdita with their puppies burst into the house. Pongo jumped on Roger and Perdita rushed to Anita.

"Why, they're Labradors!" cried Roger.

Nanny realized what had happened. "It's soot!"

"It's a miracle!" Roger exclaimed.

There were puppies everywhere. "There must be a hundred of them!" Anita cried.

Roger, Anita and Nanny started counting. "Eleven . . . thirty-six . . . forty-seven . . . sixty-five . . . eighty-four . . . one hundred and one!

"What will we do with them?" Anita asked.

Roger cried, "We'll buy a big place in the country. We'll have a Dalmatian plantation!"

Roger started singing at the piano, and Anita and the puppies joined in; they all thought this was a wonderful idea.

It was a beautiful spring morning in the forest. A squirrel woke from his sleep, stretching and yawning. A mother bird brought her babies some berries to eat. A mouse caught a dew drop to wash his face. A woodpecker popped out of his hole in a tree. The beavers sprang up from the ground to look at the day. A mother quail led her young ones along the forest floor.

Thumper, a cheerful baby rabbit, rushed towards Friend Owl, who was sleeping peacefully in his hole. "Wake up, Friend Owl!"

Friend Owl woke up with a start. "Er . . . hey! What's going on around here?" He shuffled out crossly onto a tree branch.

Thumper called excitedly, "The new prince is born! Come on, you'd better hurry up!"

All the animals—the birds, the rabbits, the beavers, the mice, the quails and Friend Owl—tiptoed through the thicket. There, resting together, was a mother deer and her baby fawn.

"Ahh," sighed the animals.

"Well," chuckled Friend Owl, "this is quite an occasion. Congratulations!" he said to the mother deer.

"Thank you very much," the mother deer replied. "Wake up," she nudged her baby.

The fawn raised his head and looked around shyly at the animals. Friend Owl fluttered his eyes playfully at the little fawn, who ducked his head.

The baby fawn tried to stand up, slowly putting weight on his slender legs, which threatened to collapse beneath him.

"Look! He's trying to get up!" called Thumper. "Kind of wobbly, isn't he?"

The fawn yawned, exhausted with this effort, and snuggled closer to his mother.

"He's getting sleepy," noticed Friend Owl. "I think it's time we all left."

Quietly, the animals began to leave. But Thumper turned back and asked the mother deer, "What are you going to call him?"

She thought carefully for a minute. "Well, I think I'll call him Bambi."

"Hmm, Bambi. I guess that will do alright," Thumper agreed.

Bambi and his mother nuzzled together, while a proud stag watched over them from a cliff above.

When Bambi was a little steadier on his feet, his mother took him for a walk through the forest. They passed many friends, who stopped to greet Bambi. They met Mrs. Quail and her children, who wished the young prince a good morning. They passed Mrs. Opossum and her family hanging upside down. Then they bumped into the rabbits.

Thumper was concerned when Bambi fell over. "He doesn't walk very well, does he?"

Mrs. Rabbit looked sternly at Thumper. "What did your father tell you this morning?"

Thumper sighed, and then recited. "If you can't say something nice, then don't say anything at all."

Bambi struggled to his feet. "Come on, get up, Bambi. Try again," Thumper and his sisters encouraged Bambi. He followed them through a hollow log. Thumper began to thump his back foot on the log. "I'm thumping!" he said proudly. "That's why they call me Thumper!"

Bambi looked up curiously as a couple of baby birds began to sing above them. "Those are birds," Thumper explained.

"Bur-bur!" copied Bambi.

With Thumper's help, Bambi began to talk, repeating words after him.

"Butterfly! Flower!" Bambi said proudly, as Thumper pointed out different wonders in the forest.

Bambi buried his head in a mound of flowers, sniffing their perfume. A little skunk popped his head up. "Flower!" Bambi cried, looking at the skunk.

Thumper rolled on the ground with laughter. "That's not a flower! He's a little . . ."

The skunk interrupted. "That's alright, he can call me a flower if he wants to . . . I don't mind!" he giggled.

A flash of lightning and the sound of thunder startled Bambi and Thumper. Thumper ran home, and Bambi returned to his mother.

He huddled close to his mother in the thicket, while the rain splattered down. All the animals tried to keep dry in their homes, while the storm continued. Eventually, it calmed down to a gentle patter of rain, which lulled Bambi to sleep.

In the morning, when the storm was over, Bambi and his mother walked through the forest.

"Mother, what are we going to do today?" Bambi asked.

"I'm going to take you to the meadow," she replied.

"Meadow? What's the meadow?" Bambi asked.

His mother answered, "It's a very wonderful place. You haven't been there before because you weren't big enough."

The edge of the forest gave way to the meadow—a lovely open place to run and chase and frolic in. Bambi rushed off excitedly. But his mother leapt in front of him, blocking his way.

"Bambi!" she said seriously. "You must never rush out on the meadow. There might be danger. Out there we are unprotected. The meadow is wide and open, there are no trees and bushes to hide us so we have to be very careful."

Bambi waited while his mother checked the meadow. "Come on, Bambi, it's alright!"

Bambi loved the meadow. He ran through the grass, playfully chasing after his mother. He dashed through the stream, splashing a baby duck. He found the rabbit family, nibbling on some clover.

"Why don't you try some?" suggested Thumper to Bambi. "No, no, not the green stuff, just eat the blossoms, that's the good stuff."

Mrs. Rabbit looked at Thumper. "What did your father tell you?"

Thumper began to chant, "Eating greens is a special treat—it makes long ears and great big feet." Then he whispered to Bambi, "But it sure is awful stuff to eat."

At the meadow stream, Bambi discovered his reflection in the water. But he noticed there were two images. Surprised, he looked up and saw another fawn. She smiled, and edged towards him. But Bambi was a little afraid, and moved backwards. She came closer. Bambi turned around and raced to his mother.

The fawn followed him, where her mother was waiting too.

Bambi's mother looked encouragingly at him. "That's little Faline," she said. Bambi tucked himself behind his mother.

"You're not afraid, are you?" said his mother, as she pushed him towards Faline. Bambi shook his head, and managed to mutter "Hello!" to Faline.

She pranced around, and Bambi scampered after her.

A group of bucks, the male deer, bounded through the meadow. Bambi and Faline stopped playing to watch them.

They seemed very large and strong to Bambi. He looked at one stag in particular, who moved with dignity and grace. This stag stopped to look at Bambi for a moment.

When the stags had passed, Bambi asked his mother, "Why was everyone still when he came on the meadow?"

"Everyone respects him. He's very brave and very wise. That's why he's known as the Great Prince of the Forest," his mother answered.

Suddenly, there was a change in the meadow. The birds flew swiftly across to the forest, warning the animals with their cries. The stags began to run from the meadow.

"Bambi!" called his mother anxiously.

But Bambi was caught up in the midst of all the animals, who were hurriedly trying to leave the meadow. "Mother," he cried desperately, looking around for her.

The proud stag came to his rescue, nodding for Bambi to follow him. They raced across the meadow, and his mother joined them, all three running rapidly towards the forest. Gunshots sounded over the meadow.

Eventually, Bambi's mother cautiously made her way out of the bushes where they had been hiding.

"Come on out, Bambi. It's safe now," she said.

"What happened, mother? Why did we all run?" Bambi asked in confusion. She replied seriously, "Man was in the forest."

Gradually, spring and summer blended into fall, with all of its wonderful colored leaves. And then fall became winter.

Bambi woke one morning to find that the forest had changed color. "What's all that white stuff?" he asked his mother.

"Snow!" she replied. "Yes, winter has come."

Bambi found it difficult to walk in the snow at first, and even more difficul to move on the frozen pond. But Thumper soon taught him how to keep his balance.

Flower, the little skunk, was not interested in playing in the snow. He was sleeping peacefully in his burrow.

"Wake up, wake up, wake up, Flower," Thumper called. "What are you doing? Hibernating?"

Flower just nodded, covered himself with his tail, and went back to sleep

While there were wonderful winter games to play, it was hard to find food. Bambi's mother found him some bark to eat, but often it was not enough.

"Winter sure is long, isn't it?" Bambi said.

"It seems long, but it won't last forever," his mother replied.

Bambi's mother found him some fresh green grass to eat, growing in the middle of a snowy meadow.

But a sound alerted Bambi's mother to danger. "Bambi," she whispered. "Quick, the thicket."

Bambi obeyed instantly, and bounded out of the meadow.

A gunshot rang out across the meadow. "Faster, faster, Bambi," his mother urged.

At the edge of the forest, Bambi charged through. Another shot was fired Bambi kept going, past the large trees, under a log, into the thicket.

He panted, "We made it, we made it, mother, we . . . mother?"

But there was no answer from his mother.

Bambi pushed back out of the thicket. He couldn't see his mother. He wandered around the trees, calling to her.

"Mother? Mother?" Bambi cried out in fear.

Bambi stopped short. There in front of him was the proud stag.

He spoke to Bambi. "Your mother can't be with you any more. Come, my son," he gestured, and he turned around.

Bambi slowly followed his father, while the snow continued to fall.

It was not long before the trees were full of singing birds again, announcing the arrival of spring.

The birds woke Friend Owl with their singing. "Oh, what now?" He tried to shoo the birds away, but they ignored him.

"Same thing, every spring. Tweet tweet, tweet tweet," he complained.

"Hello, Friend Owl! Don't you remember me?" called a voice from below Friend Owl's tree.

"Why, it's the young prince! Bambi! You've traded in your spots for a pair of antlers!" Friend Owl noticed.

"Hello, Bambi!" called a voice from the ground. "Remember me?" the voice asked, as he thumped vigorously on a log.

"Thumper?" cried Bambi.

"Hi, fellows!" giggled a skunk, who crept up to join them.

"Flower!" said Bambi and Thumper together.

The friends, all grown up now, laughed together, as a pair of birds twittered around them.

"What's the matter with them?" wondered Flower.

Friend Owl began to laugh. "They're twitterpated!" he explained.

"Twitterpated?" repeated the friends in confusion.

"Yes," Friend Owl continued. "Nearly everyone gets twitterpated in the springtime. For example, you're walking along, minding your own business, you're looking neither to the left nor to the right, when all of a sudden, you run smack bang into a pretty face."

"You begin to get weak in the knees, your head's in a whirl, and then you feel as light as a feather, and before you know it, you're walking on air."

"Gosh, that's awful!" said Thumper.

"Gee whiz!" cried Flower.

"Terrible!" agreed Bambi.

"It can happen to anyone," warned Friend Owl. "So you better be careful . . ."

"Well, it's not going to happen to me!" declared Thumper.

"Me neither!" cried Bambi.

"Me neither!" added Flower.

And the three of them marched off.

They had not gone very far before Flower heard a little giggle coming from a bush. There behind the bush was a lovely skunk. She waved at him; Flower waved back. He started to turn to follow Bambi and Thumper, but then turned back at another giggle. The two skunks bumped into each other, and accidentally kissed. Flower blushed a bright red.

"Huh! Twitterpated!" mocked Thumper, as he and Bambi continued on their walk.

But then it was Thumper's turn. A pretty rabbit saw the two friends.
She began to sing to attract Thumper's attention. He turned around.
She batted her eyes and flipped her ears. She came nearer and nearer
to Thumper, until, up close, she kissed him. Thumper thumped furiously—
he was twitterpated!

Bambi just shook his head, and continued alone.

When Bambi stopped to drink from the stream, he saw another reflection in the water.

"Hello, Bambi. Don't you remember me?" Faline asked.

Bambi was startled, and backed away, tripping himself up. Faline moved towards him and kissed him.

Then Bambi knew what Friend Owl was talking about!

Bambi and Faline pranced through the forest together. Faline disappeared into a bush, but when Bambi pushed his head through to find her, another stag glared at him from the bush. The stag pushed Bambi back and began to nudge Faline along with him.

"Bambi!" Faline called. "Bambi!"

Bambi shook his head and pawed the ground. He charged forward at the stag. The stag rushed towards him, and Bambi was thrown to the ground.

He dragged himself up, and locked horns with the stag. Faline watched in fear. Bambi fought furiously against the stag and pushed him over the cliff into the river.

Faline moved towards Bambi and nuzzled him.

It was fall when Bambi sensed that there was danger again. He left Faline sleeping in the thicket and went out into the forest to investigate.

His father found him. "Man! He is here again. Quickly, to the hills!" he warned Bambi.

Bambi went back to the thicket to find Faline, but she had already left to go looking for him.

Throughout the forest, the frightened animals began to run and hide. Gunshots rang out overhead. A small pheasant fell from the sky.

Bambi and Faline searched for each other, running deeper into the forest.

Faline dashed into a rocky canyon, where a pack of dogs saw her and began to follow her. Snarling, they chased her up a rocky ledge. Terrified, she screamed, "Bambi!"

Bambi heard Faline, and rushed to her aid. He charged at the pack of dogs, scattering them. Bambi used all his strength to fight off the dogs, kicking, bucking and charging them.

He called for Faline to jump from the ledge and run for safety, while he held the dogs back.

After Faline had fled, he rushed up the rocky incline, and escaped as rocks fell on the dogs below.

Bambi hurried after Faline, but a gunshot brought him to the ground, and he couldn't get up. He lay there, very still.

Meanwhile, the fire from the men's camp had spread to a nearby tree. It grew quickly, the fierce flames spreading through the forest.

The animals fled from the fire, which had destroyed their homes. The flames were hot and moved swiftly through the forest, burning trees and bushes and setting leaves and twigs alight.

But Bambi did not move. His father stood over him. "Get up, Bambi," he said.

Bambi struggled to get up, and eventually was able to stand. He followed his father, as they plunged through the forest, trying to escape the hot flames and burning embers.

Bambi and his father followed the river through the forest, dodging falling burning trees. At the top of the waterfall they hesitated. But they had no choice—a tree alight with flames fell behind them. In an instant, Bambi and his father jumped into the crashing, roaring water.

Eventually, they made their way to an island, where many animals had found refuge, including Faline. She and Bambi were reunited, as they looked back over the burning forest, their home.

In time, the forest grew green and lush again.

It was Thumper, with his children, who woke Friend Owl this time.

"What's going on around here?" Friend Owl asked crossly.

"It's happened!" said a baby skunk, who ran up with his father, Flower.

The animals and birds scampered, hurried, trotted and flew to the thicket, where Faline was lying. She nuzzled her two baby fawns, while the animals and birds watched admiringly.

"Prince Bambi ought to be mighty proud," said Friend Owl.

And Bambi was proud, as he stood high on the cliff, overlooking the thicket with his father.

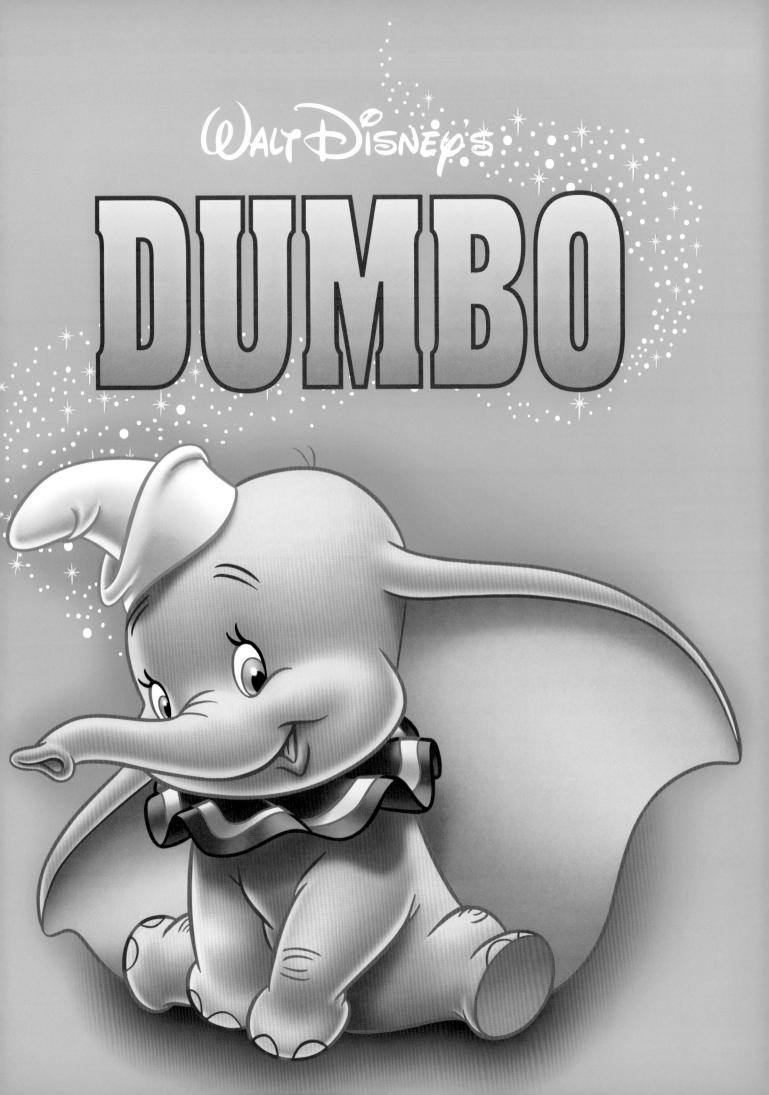

It was snowing; it was raining. The wind moaned, the lightning flashed and the thunder crashed.

As the storm began to clear, a flock of storks flew through the blue sky. But these were no ordinary storks. Each stork carried a precious bundle in its beak.

The storks flew closer to the earth—they were heading for Florida. As they descended to the ground, the storks began to drop their tightly wrapped bundles.

Many of these bundles were headed for the circus! The parcels, now attached to parachutes, floated gently into the circus.

There was a parcel for Mother Bear. She smiled in delight when the parcel sprang open to reveal a baby bear cub. Another one parachuted into Mother Bear, and a second baby bear cub rolled out to meet its mother.

Mother Kangaroo was sound asleep when her parcel arrived. Her baby joey jumped into her pouch. Mother Kangaroo was very happy to see her baby kangaroo.

There was a bundle for Mother Hippo—a baby hippo, of course. There was a new family of baby tigers for Mother and Father Tiger. Mother Giraffe loved her new baby giraffe the moment she saw it.

But poor Mrs. Jumbo looked hopefully up at the sky, wondering if there was a bundle from a stork just for her. But there was nothing.

The circus began to pack up. It was time to move on. All the animal carriages needed to be hooked up to the little train, Casey Jr. The bear family in their cage was ready to go. The kangaroos were packed into their carriage. The camels and zebras were loaded into their box. An elephant pushed the tiger family cage into position. Mother hippo and her baby plunged themselves into their tank. The giraffes could see out of the top of their carriage.

Mrs. Jumbo sadly plodded into her box, with one last glance at the sky—not a stork in sight.

The Ringmaster, hanging from the step of the caboose, called, "All aboard! All aboard!"

Casey Jr. with a huge effort, started to fire up the engine. But the cages loaded with animals were very heavy, and they jolted against each other.

With another big breath, the circus train gave a whistle, "Woo! Woo!" and pulled away from the train station.

A solitary stork, carrying a bundle in its beak, stopped flying to rest on a cloud. With a businesslike expression, he pulled out a map.

"Now, let me see," he muttered. "Must be right around here somewhere . . . I hope."

The bundle sank slowly into the cloud, while the stork checked his map. The stork quickly rescued his bundle.

"Where are we?" he asked himself, as he looked from the map to the earth below.

"Ah!" he exclaimed, as he heard a train whistle below. "That must be it! Well, little fellow, let's get going!"

He rescued his sinking bundle again and staggering under the weight, flew down towards the earth.

The stork landed on Casey Jr. and began calling out. "Mrs. Jumbo! Mrs. Jumbo! Mrs. Jumbo?"

The elephants responded. "Yoo hoo! This is the place."

The stork fluttered over to Mrs. Jumbo. He cleared his throat and recited, "Here is a baby with eyes of blue, straight from heaven right to you."

Mrs. Jumbo reached out for her bundle, but the stork thrust a clipboard in front of her. "Sign here, please." Mrs. Jumbo wrote an "X" on the paper with her trunk.

The stork sang happy birthday to the bundle, but paused at the line, "Happy birthday, dear . . . What's his name?"

"Jumbo Junior," Mrs. Jumbo answered shyly.

She unwrapped the bundle, and there inside was the dearest baby elephant.

The elephants cooed, "Isn't he adorable?"

Matriarch, the largest elephant, leaned down, and tickled Jumbo Junior. "Kootchy kootchy kootchy koo!"

Jumbo Junior sneezed, and his ears flapped out. But they were no ordinary baby elephant ears. Jumbo Junior's ears were so large that they dangled down to his feet, and nearly covered him entirely.

The elephants gasped.

"Look at those ears! Aren't they funny?" laughed Giggles, as she picked up one of Jumbo Junior's ears with her trunk.

Mrs. Jumbo slapped her away, and moved protectively towards her baby.

"What a temper! After all, who cares about her precious little Jumbo?" sniffed Prissy.

"Jumbo—you mean Dumbo!" Catty smirked.

Casey Jr. puffed valiantly as he struggled up the hill, pulling his heavy load of animals behind him. "I think I can, I think I can," he told himself as he moved up the steep hill. "I thought I could, I thought I could," he said with relief, as he rushed down the other side.

When Casey Jr. stopped at the town where the circus would be staying, it was raining heavily. But the circus needed to be set up. So it was up to the elephants and the circus men to set up the big circus tent. Even Dumbo helped to hammer the stakes into the ground.

The show was nearly ready to start. There were people crowding around the animals, including Mrs. Jumbo and Dumbo. Dumbo smiled when he heard the children's voices—he didn't understand that they were laughing at his big ears.

"Isn't that the funniest looking thing you ever saw?" mocked a skinny boy.

Mrs. Jumbo tried to move Dumbo away from him, but the boy reached past her and pulled one of Dumbo's ears back, hurting him.

Mrs. Jumbo's trunk reached for the boy and flung him over a rope. The children shouted for help, as Mrs. Jumbo began to throw hay at them.

The Ringmaster used his whip on Mrs. Jumbo, but she edged away. He called for help, and the circus men came running out with chains and poles. Dumbo tried to stay out of the way, but one of the circus men grabbed him.

At this, Mrs. Jumbo bellowed loudly and tried to reach after Dumbo with her trunk. But the circus men had chained her feet, and she couldn't move. She picked the Ringmaster up with her trunk and threw him into a bucket of water. The Ringmaster was furious.

The Ringmaster locked Mrs. Jumbo away by herself. The sign on the outside of the car read "Danger. Mad elephant."

The rest of the elephants sniggered to themselves.

"I think she went a bit too far," said Prissy. "Oh well, I suppose that's mother love."

"Well, just the same, I can't help laughing at his ears," said Giggles.

Just then, a little mouse appeared from inside a popcorn bag. "What's the matter with his ears?" wondered Timothy the mouse, looking at Dumbo all by himself in a corner.

The elephants decided to ignore Dumbo, and formed a closed circle, blocking him out.

"Giving him the cold shoulder, poor little guy. There he goes, without a friend in the world," Timothy said, watching Dumbo walk away sadly.

He decided to give the elephants a fright and jumped in amongst them.

"A mouse!" screamed Catty, and the elephants screeched and tried to jump off the floor.

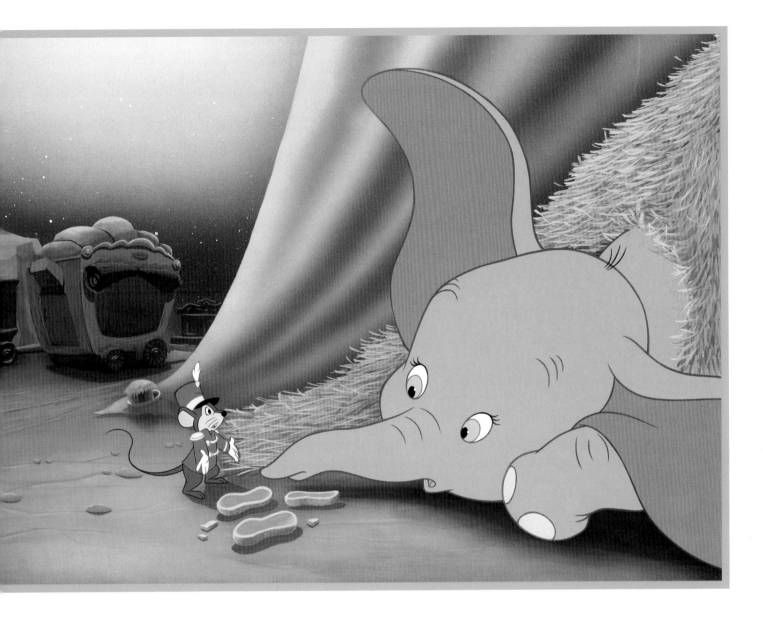

Timothy found Dumbo hiding inside a haystack. "You can come out now," Timothy called. There was no response from Dumbo.

"Look, Dumbo, I'm your friend," Timothy pleaded.

Timothy pulled some peanuts out of his hat and coaxed Dumbo out with them. "Gee, Dumbo, I think your ears are beautiful!" he said.

Timothy decided that he needed to plan an act for Dumbo, one that would make him famous. "If you're famous, they don't make fun of you," he pointed out.

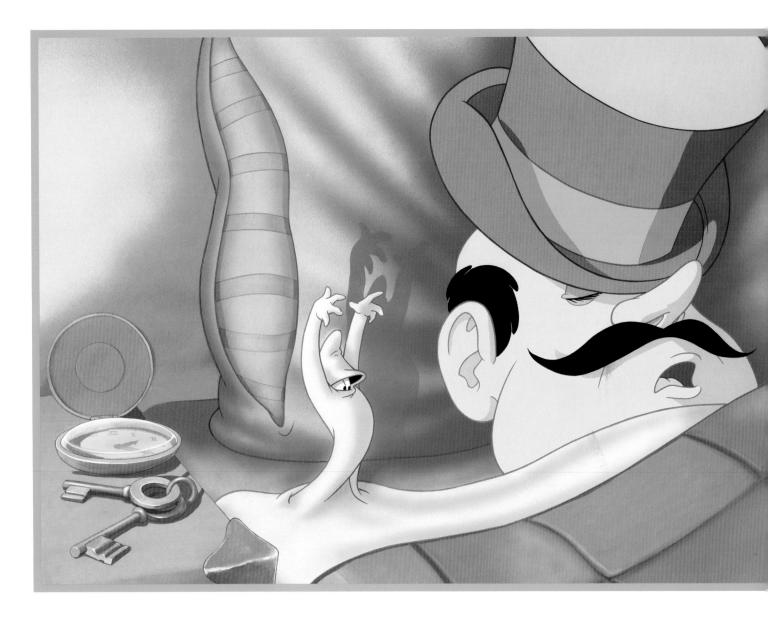

At that moment, the Ringmaster walked by, talking to one of the circus men about his great idea. "... finally all seventeen elephants have constructed an enormous pyramid ..." he planned. But he couldn't work out the ending for the elephant act.

Timothy had his own great idea. That night, when the Ringmaster was sleeping, Timothy whispered in his ear. The next morning, the Ringmaster knew how his elephant pyramid would end.

In the big circus tent, the Ringmaster stood surrounded by the elephants. "Ladies and gentlemen, we will now present for your entertainment the most stupendous, magnificent, super-colossal spectacle!"

Matriarch put her front feet on a ball. Prissy climbed on top of Matriarch. Catty pulled herself on top of Prissy. Prissy groaned. "Gaining a little weight, aren't you, honey?"

Catty lowered her trunk to help lift Giggles onto the pyramid. One by one, the elephants managed to push, climb, squeeze or clamber themselves on top of each other.

Inside the dressing room, Timothy tied up Dumbo's ears so they wouldn't trip him up. And then he pushed him out into the circus arena.

The Ringmaster announced, "And now I present the world's smallest little elephant, who will spring from this springboard in one spring to the top of this pyramid waving his little flag for a grand climax. Ladies and gentlemen, I give you . . . Dumbo!"

Dumbo burst into the arena, heading determinedly for the springboard. But his ears loosened, and he tripped over them. He missed the springboard and dived into the ball underneath the balancing elephants!

The elephants struggled to stay together. Prissy bounced on the platform, which broke, and sent her flying. Giggles and Catty landed on the trapeze bicycle and cycled frantically across the tightrope wire. The ropes broke, and the elephants fell into the crowd. The big tent started to collapse, while people ran everywhere, trying to get out.

As a punishment, Dumbo was made a clown. He was dressed up as a baby, put up the top of a burning house, and the frightened baby elephant was made to jump down into a net held by clowns dressed as firefighters. Dumbo was terribly unhappy.

But the clowns were pleased with their new act and celebrated by drinking lemonade. When they left their tent, they didn't even notice they had knocked the lemonade bottle into a bucket.

Timothy tried to cheer Dumbo up. "We're going over to see your mother!"

Mrs. Jumbo was chained in her car, but she could stretch her trunk out the window and cradle Dumbo. They clung together, until Timothy gently led Dumbo away.

Dumbo cried as he slowly walked back to the tent. His sobs led to hiccups, so Timothy suggested he have a little drink from a bucket of water nearby. Only it was no bucket of water—it was the bucket of lemonade left by the clowns!

Timothy decided to test this water as Dumbo continued to hiccup. He fell right in, and started to sing to himself. He floated out of the bucket on a lemonade bubble.

Dumbo started to blow bubbles—little ones, square ones, big ones— even bubbles that seemed to turn into pink elephants! Dumbo and Timothy watched in amazement as the elephant bubbles appeared to dance across the sky.

It was morning. A group of crows sat on a branch of a tall tree, scratching their heads. "Well, I just can't believe my eyes," one of them said, looking down the tree.

A big crow flew in to them. "Come on, step aside, brother. What's cooking?"

The big crow took a look down the tree. There lay Dumbo, with Timothy on top of him, asleep—in the tree!

He flew down to them. Timothy woke up. "What are you boys doing down here?"

The big crow spluttered. "What are we doing down here? I suppose you and the elephant aren't doing anything up in this tree?"

Timothy repeated, "Tree?" He looked down and gasped.

Timothy clung frantically to Dumbo's trunk. "Dumbo! Dumbo! Don't look now, but I think we're up in a tree!"

Dumbo slowly opened his eyes, looked around, looked down— and fell.

The crows laughed as Dumbo and Timothy fell into a pond.

Timothy and Dumbo began to make their way back to the circus.

Timothy started to think. "I wonder how we ever got up in that tree. Now let's see. Elephants can't climb trees, can they? No, that's ridiculous. Couldn't jump up. Mmm, it's too high."

"Hey there, son. Maybe you all flew up!" the big crow said as he laughed scornfully.

"Maybe we flew up," Timothy repeated slowly.

"That's it!" he exclaimed. "Dumbo! You flew! Your ears. Just look at them, Dumbo. They're the perfect wings. The very things that held you down are going to carry you up and up! I can see it all now. Dumbo! The ninth wonder of the universe, the world's only flying elephant!"

The crows began to make fun of Dumbo and Timothy. "Ha, ha! Elephants don't fly."

Timothy was mad. "You ought to be ashamed of yourselves, a bunch of guys like you, picking on a poor little guy like him. How would you like to be left alone in the cold, cruel, heartless world? Why, just because he's got those big ears . . ."

The crows apologized for teasing Dumbo, and agreed to help him. They got together to work out a plan.

The big crow gave Timothy a feather. "Use the magic feather," he told him.

"Now you can fly!" Timothy said, as he gave the magic feather to Dumbo.

Dumbo tottered on the edge of a cliff. Timothy was perched in Dumbo's hat. The crows were behind Dumbo, pushing him with all their might. Dumbo was scared.

He started to flap his ears, as Timothy encouraged him. "Faster! Faster! Get up to flying speed! Take off!"

Dumbo continued to flap his ears, still looking scared. Timothy sighed and said, "Oh, it's no use, Dumbo."

But Timothy and Dumbo didn't realize that Dumbo was indeed flying! They soared through the sky, with the crows flapping beside them.

"Dumbo! I knew you could do it!" exclaimed Timothy proudly.

It was show time again, and time for the clowns. Dumbo was dressed as a baby again, and was put at the top of the burning building. The firefighter clowns were running around, pretending to put out the fire.

"Got the magic feather?" Timothy whispered from Dumbo's hat.

At the signal from the clowns, Dumbo took off, as if he was going to fall into the net held by the clowns below.

Suddenly, Dumbo lost his grip on the magic feather. Startled, he continued to fall, and Timothy was worried. "Dumbo, come on fly; open up those ears."

Timothy pleaded with Dumbo, as they both moved faster and faster towards the ground. "The magic feather was just a joke. You can fly, honestly," urged Timothy.

All of a sudden, Dumbo flapped his ears out, and swooped low over the net, zooming up into the air. The audience was amazed. So was the Ringmaster.

Timothy was excited. "We did it, we did it!" he shouted.

Dumbo soared around the tent and then dived down. He had great fun chasing the clowns, who scattered in all directions, even into the water barrel! Dumbo flew after the man selling peanuts and scooped up all the peanuts from his cart. He sprayed the peanuts at the elephants, who could not believe their eyes.

"You're making history," noted Timothy.

And he did. All the newspapers printed stories about Dumbo, and Timothy became famous too.

Soon, it was time for the circus to move on again. Casey Jr. was ready to go.

This time, there was a special carriage at the end of the train. The sign said "Dumbo—private."

As Casey pulled the train along, Dumbo flew into his carriage, and there inside was Mrs. Jumbo!